Hare and the Big Green Lawn

BY KATHARINE CRAWFORD ROBEY ILLUSTRATED BY LARRY MacDOUGALL

RISING MOON

www.risingmoonbooks.com

Text © 2006 by Katharine Crawford Robey
Illustrations © 2006 by Larry MacDougall

www.risingmoonbooks.com

Composed in the United States of America
Printed in China

Edited by Theresa Howell
Designed by Katie Jennings

FIRST IMPRESSION 2006

ISBN 10: 0-87358-889-4
ISBN 13: 978-0-87358-889-8

10   09   08   07   06   5   4   3   2   1

Library of Congress Cataloging-in-Publication Data Pending

To my mother,
Eleanor Crawford Uehling,
who showed me wildflowers before anything else.
–K.C.R.

The work in this book is dedicated to my wife, Patricia,
whose continuous love, help, and support
make my life a joyous adventure.
–L.M.

Hare moved away from the country.
He took the smallest house, with the biggest
lawn, at the end of the street.
   He liked his little house. But why was his
yard short and bright green, nothing like home?
"This must be fixed," Hare said to himself.

"You've got the biggest lawn," said Skunk, spraying
water on her own yard. "Better take care."

"I will," Hare replied. He thought he knew how.
He hopped high over the grass as if he didn't want to
touch it. Then he busied himself moving in.

The high spring sun beat down on everyone's grass.

Hare's neighbors, Skunk, Bobcat, and Raven, watered their lawns and got hot.

Hare stayed in the shade of an umbrella and kept cool.
His grass wilted and turned brown, but he didn't mind.
He waited and hoped, hoped and waited.

Short blinding rain came, and Hare's grass disappeared into mud. He rolled around in the cool goo and chuckled. Was it muddy enough?

Oh, how the neighbors stared!

The mud dried. Wild plants popped up in
Hare's big, brown lawn. Sagebrush, bluestem,
June grass—no need to water them. They grew tall.
But were they straggly enough?

Hare was sweeping his walk when the sagebrush parted.
"You've got weeds," Bobcat growled.

Hare smiled.

Wind swept over the neighborhood. It reached
Hare's straggly, weedy lawn. Tiny seeds settled in.
More rain fell.

"Not much," thought Hare, watching from
the window. "But enough."

He crossed his paws for luck.

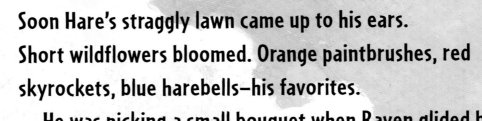

Soon Hare's straggly lawn came up to his ears.
Short wildflowers bloomed. Orange paintbrushes, red
skyrockets, blue harebells—his favorites.

He was picking a small bouquet when Raven glided by.
"What a big mess!" she croaked.

She gave him the eye just as a breeze carried her
back to her lawn.

Hare hopped happily through his big, messy yard to
his house. How beautiful the little bouquet looked on his
kitchen table.

Time passed.

Skunk, Bobcat, and Raven watered
and clipped, clipped and watered.

Meanwhile Hare swayed in a hammock
and dozed.

Then one day, Hare's nose began to twitch with excitement. It twitched some more. He opened his eyes and stared at what had happened to his big yard.

It had changed for good!

He swung from his hammock, thumped out the news, and leapt for joy.

Hare felt at home.

Skunk, Bobcat, and Raven saw
Hare thump and leap.
They stopped clipping.
Suddenly, everything was quiet.
They looked out over Hare's big yard.
What a surprise!

It was no longer messy or weedy or straggly or
muddy and brown, and certainly not bright green.

They sniffed the air and left their lawns. Up
Hare's path they came.

"We came to say," began Bobcat. A lizard slid by.

"We need to say," croaked Raven. A cricket sang.

Skunk took an important breath. "That scent. I
still know it. Sweet sagebrush," she said.

"Hare, this isn't a lawn anymore. What is it?"
Bobcat and Raven leaned in close.

"It's a meadow!" Hare replied.

"Ahh," they said.

Skunk sunk her nose into the sagebrush. Bobcat batted at a butterfly. Raven remembered that she could sing.

Hare's big yard was full of sagebrush and waving grass and wildflowers. Butterflies fluttered. Bees buzzed.

They'd all known a meadow like this—Skunk, Bobcat, and Raven. But that was long before Hare moved in. They'd forgotten how much they loved it.

Until now.

The sun set. The hammock swayed. Up
from Hare's big, silver meadow, fireflies
rose and twinkled like tiny stars.
It was peaceful there.

HOW TO GROW YOUR OWN MEADOW

Have you ever seen a field of wildflowers?

In the story, Hare comes from a place just like that, where all sorts of flowers and plants live naturally. No one has to grow them. The plants that pop up in Hare's yard are native to many western prairies. They live just fine without any help from people. They don't need water or fertilizer or mowing or clipping. They like the weather just the way it is.

You can make part of your yard into a meadow like Hare's. Start with bare soil. Next, plant wildflowers and native grasses or seeds that come from the country-side near your home. Ask your local garden center or a garden club where you can buy meadow plants or seeds. Then plant carefully. Follow the directions.

Since you're starting a new meadow, you may need to water a little at first. Once your plants have taken root, sit back and watch and wait like Hare did. You won't have to mow or clip, except once a year.

You can find books that tell more about growing wild meadows or using native plants. Look in the gardening section of bookstores or on the Web.

Who knows? After your meadow grows, you might see Hare hopping happily about in your own yard.